COLLETTE'S MAGIC STAR

BAKERS' DOZEN
#3

COLLETTE'S MAGIC STAR
Suzanne Weyn

A
LITTLE APPLE
PAPERBACK

SCHOLASTIC INC.
New York Toronto London Auckland Sydney

ISBN 0-590-43562-0

12 11 10 9 8 7 6 5 4 3 2 1   1 2 3 4 5 6/9

Printed in the U.S.A.   28

First Scholastic printing, November 1991

1

Halloween

COLLETTE BAKER stood in the front hall-way and tugged on her tail. It was on tight. She tucked her thick, black braid into her hat with the cat ears sewn onto it. The whiskers she'd glued to her dark skin itched, but it was worth it. She was very, very pleased with her cat costume.

Her eleven adopted brothers and sisters ran around upstairs getting their costumes together. She could hear their voices from downstairs.

"Who took my tape?"

"Has anyone seen my snake bracelet?"

"*Yuggghhh!* Someone put a rubber bug in my wig!"

Mrs. Baker hurried down the stairs. She wore a tall, pointed witch hat and a heavy black cloak. A small clown wearing a big blue wig followed behind her. "You look great!" Collette told three-year-old Dixie.

With a wide grin, Dixie honked the round red nose tied over her own nose.

"Have you seen Jack?" Mrs. Baker asked Collette.

Creak! The closet door opened a crack, and a hideous face with long fangs and purple eyes peered out at them.

Roar! cried the monster, leaping into the hallway.

"There's Jack," shouted Dixie, pointing at the monster.

Five-year-old Jack lifted the paper-bag mask from his head. He looked disappointed. "How did you know it was me?" he asked.

2

Dixie shrugged and honked her nose again.

"You fooled *me,*" said Collette. "I was super-scared."

Jack smiled and put back the mask he'd made in kindergarten.

"Let's get in the van, kids," said Mrs. Baker. She led them to the door, shouting as she went. "Attention everybody! If you want to go trick-or-treating, get in the van. Another five minutes and I'm leaving!"

The Bakers lived in the country. The houses were far apart, so the kids had to be driven from door-to-door.

As Collette headed out to the van, eight-year-old Hilary pranced down the stairs. She was dressed as Cleopatra. Tossing her long, brown hair, she lifted her slightly pointy nose. "You're *not* going trick-or-treating, I hope," she said.

"Why shouldn't I?" asked Collette.

"We're eight years old," said Hilary. "That's much too old for trick-or-treating."

"Then why are you all dressed up?" asked Jack.

"I'm going to the school Halloween party later. But I wouldn't be caught dead trick-or-treating," said Hilary. Wild Falls elementary always held a big Halloween party in the gym on Halloween night.

"You're not too old to trick-or-treat," Mrs. Baker disagreed, spreading her cape. "I'm going."

"It's not the same," Hilary insisted. "You're not actually trick-or-treating. Besides, when you're really old, people know that you're not being babyish."

"Who's really old?" came a jolly voice from the kitchen. In the next second Grannie Baker stepped into the hallway. Wide, shimmery pants ballooned around her legs. Red velvet slippers curled at her toes like elf shoes. In front of her face she held a frightening mask. "How do you like the costume?" she asked. "I picked it up in Bali on my last trip." Grannie Baker was always traveling.

4

"It's cool," said Collette.

"It *is* nice, in a weird sort of way," agreed Hilary, walking regally off into the living room. "Would you check my makeup?" Hilary asked sixteen-year-old Chris, who sat on the couch reading her copy of *Teen Today* magazine.

"Sure," said Chris, who was dressed as a vampire. She was waiting for some friends. They were going to a Halloween party at the teen center.

On the living room floor sat twelve-year-old Mark dressed as a hobo. He was busy tying a bandanna around Jojo's neck. Jojo was the family's big, black Labrador retriever, but tonight he was posing as a hobo's dog.

Mark and his friends would meet up and simply run around hitting one another with chalk and globs of shaving cream.

Collette couldn't wait to be big enough to do that.

"Mom," Mrs. Baker said to Grannie, "all

the candy is in this top drawer. When it starts to get dark, turn on the light over the door and the front lamp."

"No problemo," said Grannie. "I have this trick-or-treating thing under control."

"Mommy!" whined Dixie. "I want to trick-or-treat!"

"Where *are* those kids?" sighed Mrs. Baker. She steered Jack and Dixie out the door. "Better decide what you want to do," she told Collette.

"I'll just go to the Halloween party later," Collette told her mother.

"Are you sure?" asked Mrs. Baker.

Collette nodded. She wouldn't enjoy herself now. She'd feel dumb and babyish. Thanks to Hilary.

"Okay," said Mrs. Baker. "Dad will be home in time to drive you to the party. And as for the rest of these slowpokes . . ." Mrs. Baker turned to Grannie. "Watch this," she said with a wink. "Goodbye!" Mrs. Baker called. Then . . .

Slam! Mrs. Baker slammed the door shut as she went out.

Just as Mrs. Baker expected, the sound of the slamming door brought the kids running. First came seven-year-old Howie in his ninja outfit, followed by six-year-old Kevin, also dressed as a ninja. (Kevin always did everything Howie did.) "Wait for us!" they cried, tearing out the front door.

Seven-year-old Terry appeared next, dragging her mermaid tail along. She hurried out the front door.

"Did she leave yet?" cried eight-year-old Patty as she thundered down the stairs. The brim of her baseball cap flopped in her eyes. She was dressed as a ball player.

Behind Patty was Olivia, who was also eight. She moved slowly, trying not to tear the tinfoil out of which she'd made her astronaut costume. Olivia dreamed of someday going into outer space and had dressed as an astronaut for the last three Halloweens.

"Better hurry," said Grannie. "I hear the motor running."

Olivia hopped anxiously on the stairs. "Patty, tell Mom to wait. I can't run in this costume."

"Okay," said Patty from the doorway.

"You're trick-or-treating?" Collette questioned Olivia.

"Sure I am," said Olivia. "Aren't you?"

"Don't you think we're too old?" Collette asked.

Olivia looked in at Hilary, who was polishing her nails in the living room. "Don't listen to her. It'll be fun," said Olivia.

"I think I'll just wait for the party," Collette replied.

The horn outside honked impatiently. "Well, I'm going," said Olivia as she scurried to the door with small, careful steps.

As Olivia left, six trick-or-treaters arrived at the Bakers' doorstep. They were dressed as cans of soda, and lined up in six-pack formation as they stood at the door. "Very clever," chuckled Grannie, tossing each of them candy.

Collette turned toward the kitchen. Someone had left the cellar door open. It blocked her path. *I wonder who's down there,* thought Collette, peeking around the door.

Suddenly a big, furry spider fell into her face.

"*Aaaahhh!*" shrieked Collette, more startled than scared.

"*Hahahaha!*" laughed Kenny, running up the cellar steps. "Scared you!" A ghoulish rubber horror mask covered his face. He pulled the mask off, revealing a handsome face with light brown skin and dark, merry eyes.

"You did not," Collette insisted. She picked up the spider. It was attached to a string and tacked to the top of the ceiling. It had been sitting on top of the door. When she moved the door, the spider fell in her face.

"Hey, cool costume," Kenny commented. "A black cat."

Collette wiggled her tail at him. "Aren't you trick-or-treating?" she asked. He was also eight.

"Naw," Kenny replied.

"Me neither," said Collette. "Eight is too old, isn't it?"

"I don't care about that," said Kenny scornfully. "I stayed behind because I've got my Halloween trick working perfectly. The next kids who come to this house are going to be scared out of their wits." His eyes were bright with mischievous laughter.

Collette leaned forward eagerly. Kenny always thought up the funniest pranks. "Tell me. Tell me," she said.

Kenny checked to make sure no one was listening. Then he whispered his plan into Collette's ear.

As Collette listened, her hand flew to her mouth. "I don't know, Kenny," she said. "That sounds too dangerous."

2

The Dangerous Trick

A DAMP BREEZE sent a shiver up Collette's back. She wrapped her arms around herself. The sun was orange and low in the sky. The trees in the forest behind her threw quivering, fingery shadows everywhere. It would soon be dark.

Collette looked up into the elm tree near the Bakers' garage. "Make sure it's tight," she called to Kenny, who sat on a branch midway up the tree.

"It's real tight," Kenny shouted down. His ghost costume was draped beside him

11

over the branch. "Stop being all worried. I've been planning this trick for months."

That was true enough. Collette had seen Kenny try out other versions of this trick as he prepared for Halloween. His first attempt had been back in August. He'd made a giant dummy and tied it to a rope.

Collette remembered that day clearly. It was the first day Patty came to the Bakers' from her foster home. She pulled up in the car driven by the social worker and *whap!* The dummy had slipped from Kenny's hands and landed with a thud on the hood of the car.

Poor Patty, thought Collette, remembering how pale Patty had looked when she got out of the car. *What a way to be greeted by your new family.*

Over the next month, Kenny had experimented with several other versions of the trick. He tried attaching a lighter dummy to a Slinky coil, but the coil kept slipping off.

He wanted to drop the neighbors' black cat from the Slinky, but his sisters threatened to lock him in a closet and report him to the ASPCA if he tried such a thing.

This was the first time, though, that Kenny himself planned to swing down on the rope.

"It'll be great," he'd told her in the hallway. "I've cut a slit in my ghost costume. The rope will go through it so no one will see my hands holding on." His ghost costume was a white sheet with the horrible mask over his face.

"I'll jump off the branch and swing out. I'll look like a ghost flying around. It'll scare everybody silly," he continued excitedly.

"How will you get back into the tree?" Collette had asked.

"Simple. I just climb back up the rope."

There was probably nothing to worry about, Collette told herself. Kenny was always climbing trees. There was a whole forest just behind the Bakers' house. Kenny had built three different tree houses and never hurt himself.

And she knew Kenny could swing on a rope. During the summer, the family had spent the day swimming and picnicking at Wild Falls. (These were the waterfalls the town was named after.) There was a small but deep lake at the bottom of one of the falls. Someone had tied a rope to an over-hanging tree. Kenny was the first to swing out on the rope and jump off in the middle of the lake. Mark and Chris had also tried. The rest of the Baker kids had been too scared.

Collette sighed. There was no way she could stop Kenny even if she wanted to. She couldn't tell on him. *No tattling* was the first rule among the Baker kids.

A blue car stopped at the end of the Bakers' long driveway. Five kids in costumes piled out and headed up the drive.

"Aha, my first victims," said Kenny glee-fully.

Quickly, he pulled on his ghost costume. Then he pulled the rope into the opening in the white sheet.

"At least let them get their candy first," said Collette.

"Good idea," Kenny agreed. "That way they won't tell Grannie on me."

The kids were nearing the tree. Collette tried to see who they were under their costumes. She thought she recognized the Fitzwater twins. They were in the second grade. Today they were dressed as Tweedledee and Tweedledum from *Through the Looking-Glass*.

The trick-or-treaters got their candy and were returning to the car. "Here they come," Collette alerted Kenny in a quiet voice.

Kenny waited on his branch until the kids were directly under the tree.

Booooooo! Boo! Boo! Booooooooooooooooooooooo! Kenny sailed down out of the tree high above their heads. His white sheet fluttered behind him. In the half-light it was hard to see the rope. He really did appear to be flying.

Ahhhhhhhhhhhhhhhhhhhhhhhhhh! The terrified kids ran shrieking back to their car. After a moment, the car drove away.

When the rope stopped swinging, Kenny scrambled back up to his branch.

"Did you see them?" gasped Collette, doubled over with laughter. "Man! Were they scared stiff!"

Kenny bounced happily on the branch. "That was so cool!" he shouted. "All right! I can't wait to do it again."

He didn't have to wait long. A tan station wagon nosed its way into the driveway. Nine kids got out, dragging their candy bags beside them.

Once again, Kenny waited until after the kids had gotten their candy. Then, when they neared the tree, Kenny swung down over them. *Boo! Boo! Boo! Boooooo-oooooo!*

The kids screamed and ran to their car.

But this time the car didn't leave. A small woman with bright red curly hair got out of the car. "What is the meaning of this?" bellowed a familiar voice.

Uh-oh, thought Collette, sucking in her breath. It was Mrs. Arnold, the lunch monitor at school, and the meanest woman at Wild Falls elementary. One of those kids must have been Lizzie, her daughter.

Collette's first thought was to run away. But she couldn't leave Kenny there all alone. So she stood, frozen, by the tree.

Kenny was as stunned as Collette. He hung onto the rope, swaying gently back and forth.

"That is a dangerous and frightening prank!" yelled Mrs. Arnold, standing under the tree. "I am reporting this to your parents."

"Please, Mrs. Arnold," Collette stepped forward. "We were just fooling around. We didn't mean to — "

Crack! Creeee-aaaack! Collette looked up and saw the white insides of the branch that held Kenny. It was splitting open!

"Yeeoooo! Help!" cried Kenny, kicking his feet wildly as he tried to pull himself up the rope.

Cree-aaack! The split in the branch cracked open wider.

"Don't move, young man," cried Mrs. Arnold, hurrying back to her car. "Stay very still. I have a CB radio in my car. I'll call the fire department. They'll get you down."

"Oh, my gosh! Kenny!" Collette cried, staring wide-eyed up at her brother. She could get Grannie, but she was afraid to leave Kenny. Glancing at Mrs. Arnold, she saw the woman talking into the speaker of her CB.

The next sound Collette heard pierced her ears. It was the loud snap of the branch breaking in two.

"*Aaaahhhh!*" screeched Kenny as he fell to the ground.

"Kenny! Kenny!" screamed Collette, running to him. Her heart jumped into her throat. Kenny was lying in a heap under his white sheet — and he wasn't moving.

3

At the Hospital

BE OKAY. *Be okay. Please, be okay,* Collette prayed over and over. She sat beside Hilary in the back of Grannie's red sports car. They were racing behind the ambulance that was carrying Kenny to the hospital.

In front sat Mark, looking grim. The spinning red light of the ambulance flashed on his face. Chris had stayed behind to tell the others what had happened.

"Thank goodness your father arrived in time," said Grannie as she screeched around a corner. Mr. Baker was in the ambulance with Kenny. He'd been dropped off from work just as the fire engines and ambulance were pulling up to the house. He'd raced up the driveway with the medics from the Wild Falls hospital.

"How could you let him do such a stupid thing?" Hilary hissed at Collette.

Collette shot her a deadly look. "Shut up, Hilary," she snapped.

"Be quiet," scolded Mark. "This isn't the time to fight."

Both girls were silent. Mark was right. This was serious. When they'd picked the sheet off Kenny, he was out cold. But he was breathing, and within minutes he'd opened his eyes.

Carefully, carefully, the medics had lifted him onto a stretcher.

Now Collette was so scared she felt as though she could barely breathe. Maybe Kenny would be crippled. Or maybe he would . . . die.

Oh, no. Collette pushed that thought aside. She'd seen enough death.

Her mother had died when she was born. Collette had no memory of her. But she'd seen pictures. She would study her mother's smooth dark skin and large almost-black eyes. Collette could see that she looked like her mother.

Her father had taken good care of her. Then — when Collette was six — a gas explosion at the plant where he worked had killed him. That's when she went to live with her Grandma Dupré in New Orleans.

Grandma Dupré was kind, and Collette grew to love her very much. She was old, though. And right after Christmas last year, Grandma Dupré had gotten sick and died.

Luckily for Collette, Grandma Dupré had a friend who knew Grannie Baker. That was how the Bakers came to adopt her.

Collette didn't want anything more to do with people dying. It hurt too much. The pain was too deep. No, Kenny was not going to die. Collette wouldn't let him.

Grannie followed the ambulance to the emergency entrance. She pulled her car onto the sidewalk.

"Miss, you can't park here," said a guard, coming up to the window.

Grannie got out of the car. "Give me a ticket. Have it towed. I don't care," said Grannie, hurrying over to the ambulance. The kids scrambled out of the car behind her.

"Miss, I said you'll have to move — " The guard followed them.

"This is an emergency, sonny. Can't you read the sign over the door? It says *emergency*." With a wave of her pudgy hand, Grannie shooed the guard away. To Collette's surprise, the guard left.

The medics took Kenny from the back of the ambulance. "How's he doing, Tom?" Grannie asked Mr. Baker.

Mr. Baker's wispy blond hair fluttered in the breeze. His face was pale and worried. "He's somewhat dazed," he replied. "His left arm and leg seem to be broken, too."

"Is he going to be all right?" asked Mark.

"I hope so," said Mr. Baker. "Come on."

The family hurried into the hospital. Everyone but Mr. Baker had to stay in the waiting room while the doctors checked Kenny.

Collette seated herself on the green vinyl couch. "Look, Mommy, a kitty cat," said a little girl who sat across the way. The small girl was pale. Collette could tell she was sick. She tried to smile at the girl, but her mouth wouldn't move. She didn't feel much like smiling.

Collette had almost forgotten that she was still in her costume. She looked at Mark, with his hobo outfit. Grannie had thrown a raincoat over her balloony pants. Hilary's Cleopatra makeup was smeared all over her face.

They had been waiting an hour when Mrs. Baker came charging into the emergency room. "How is he?" she asked when she spotted Grannie.

"We don't know yet," Grannie replied.

Mrs. Baker ran up to the front desk and spoke to the nurse. Then she disappeared behind a set of swinging doors. In another ten minutes, Mr. Baker came out. He looked weary and sad.

"Well?" asked Grannie, jumping to her feet.

"Besides breaking his leg and arm, he's fractured his collarbone and one rib," Mr. Baker told them.

"How horrible!" gasped Hilary.

"That's not what has me worried," Mr. Baker continued. "He may have a concussion."

"What's that?" asked Hilary.

"A head injury," Mr. Baker explained.

"Oh my gosh! Will he get better?" asked Collette.

"Sure. Sure he will," said Mr. Baker. But he didn't sound sure.

Collette wanted to believe her father. They would just have to wait and see.

4

Kenny Comes Home

"HEY! LOOK! Hailstones," said Collette, running to the living room window. Tiny white rocks bounced off the windowsill. It was mid-November, and this was the first sign of winter weather.

"Who cares," grumbled Kenny from the living room couch. The cast on his leg was propped up on the coffee table. Cloth Ace bandages were wrapped around his ribs and collarbone. His left arm was in a cast. It lay on his chest in a sling.

His eyes were open, but they'd lost their

sparkle. Kenny's vision had started to blur the day after the accident. He strained and squinted, trying to bring the blurred forms into focus. It was no use. Everything stayed hazy, no matter how hard he tried.

In the hospital, Kenny had had lots of tests. The doctors had expected his vision to clear up, but it didn't. So they ran more tests. Finally they discovered a small blood clot blocking one of the veins to Kenny's eye.

"It might just get better on its own," one of the doctors told the Bakers. "If it doesn't, we'll have to operate. Or we can just go ahead and operate right away."

Mr. Baker wanted to wait. "There's no sense putting the boy through an operation if it isn't one-hundred percent necessary," he said.

Collette settled herself cross-legged on the end of the couch. She went back to reading out loud from her geography book. Although Kenny was in the other third-grade class, he was doing the same work and using the same books as Collette's class. Collette, Patty, Hilary, and Olivia — who were all in the same third-grade class — took turns reading to him.

Olivia came in and plopped on the blue chair across from the couch. "Ready for science yet?" she asked, taking off her blue-rimmed eyeglasses and wiping them on her blouse.

"In a minute," said Collette. As she turned the page, a sheet of paper fell from her book. It was a notice about the up-coming Christmas play. Everyone in class had to get it signed. "Did you hear about the Christmas play?" Collette asked Kenny.

"Yeah, but tell me what the paper says."

Collette cleared her throat and read. "On Christmas Eve, the second and third grades will be presenting a performance of *A Christmas Carol* by Charles Dickens — "

"Is that the play about Scrooge?" Kenny interrupted.

"Uh-huh," said Collette. She went back

to reading. ". . . by Charles Dickens in the Wild Falls elementary auditorium at six P.M. At the end of the month, we will be auditioning children for the various roles. All children not receiving speaking roles will sing in the chorus. If for any reason you do not wish your child to participate, please notify us immediately. Thank you. Gladys Sherman and Alfonse Popol. Classes three-one and three-two."

"Wow! Big Al's name is really Alfonse," Kenny laughed, referring to his burly teacher. "Good thing he's big, with a name like that."

Collette and Olivia smiled. It was good to see Kenny laugh. He hadn't laughed much since the accident. Then his expression became serious. "Oh, no," he moaned. "I won't be able to act. That means I'm going to have to sing in the chorus."

"So what?" asked Collette.

Olivia sighed. "Have you ever heard Kenny sing?"

Collette tried to remember. She realized that she never had heard him. "Pretty bad, huh?" she guessed.

"Like a dying bull frog," said Hilary, as she and Patty came into the living room.

"That's *not* what I was about to say," said Olivia. "But singing isn't one of Kenny's talents."

"Maybe they'll give you a talking part, even if you are on crutches. They all know you were great in last year's play," said Olivia.

"He was the best, funniest Father Christmas you ever saw," Olivia said to Patty and Collette, who hadn't been there to see the play. "Everyone was laughing like crazy."

"I know," cried Collette. "You could play Tiny Tim. He had a crutch, and — " Collette cut herself short. From the kitchen came the sound of shouting. Mr. and Mrs. Baker were having an argument.

The kids looked at one another. Their

parents got along very well, and it was unusual for them to fight.

"Why can't you be reasonable about this!" yelled Mrs. Baker.

"I *am* being reasonable," Mr. Baker shouted back. "I just don't agree with you."

Then their voices were low again and the kids couldn't make out what was being said. "I have to hear this," said Hilary, jumping to her feet.

"Hilary!" said Patty. "You shouldn't snoop."

Hilary paid no attention. She hurried out of the room. For a moment, the kids sat, looking at one another.

Then Olivia said, "I wonder what they're fighting about."

Collette jumped up. "I'm going to find out," she said.

"Me, too," said Olivia and Patty together. At once, the girls started for the door.

"Hey, what about me?" Kenny called.

Collette went back and helped Kenny onto his crutch. Together they went to the hallway and stood behind Hilary, who was listening at the kitchen doorway.

"Tom," said Mrs. Baker. "Face facts. He's not getting better. His teacher called again today. He strongly recommended moving Kenny to a special school. His grades have dropped. He's just not keeping up."

"I think we should give it more time," Mr. Baker objected. "The doctors said his sight might get better all by itself."

"They said it *might*," Mrs. Baker reminded him. "They didn't promise that it *would*. Meanwhile, Kenny is falling behind in school."

"No," Mr. Baker said firmly. "An eye operation is very tricky. If Kenny doesn't absolutely need it, I'd rather not put him through that. Let's just wait another two weeks. Maybe he won't need an operation at all."

"I hope you're right," said Mrs. Baker, her voice dropping. "What should I tell Mr. Popol?"

"Tell him Kenny is to stay right where he is," said Mr. Baker. "He's not going to a school for the visually impaired and blind."

The word *blind* hit Collette like a hammer. She turned to see how Kenny was taking all this. He was leaning with his back against the wall. Two big tears rolled down his cheeks.

5

Grannie's Good News

"GOBBLEGOBBLEGOBBLEGOBBLE!" Dixie pretended to be a turkey. Merrily, she chased Jojo around the kitchen.

"Whoa, there," laughed Mr. Baker, standing by the oven. "Slow down. I have to baste this turkey and I don't want you sliding into the open oven door. It's hot."

"Okay, Daddy," Dixie said, breathless from running.

Collette watched this scene and smiled. She and Terry sat at the table peeling sweet potatoes. As Mr. Baker opened the oven, the warm smell of roasting turkey filled the kitchen. Collette loved Thanksgiving.

Grannie Baker came in, bakery boxes balanced in her arms. She wore a beautiful lavender cape that came to the floor.

"That's a pretty cape," said Terry.

"I picked this up in Ireland," Grannie said, setting her boxes on the table. "Want to try it on?"

"Could I?" cried Terry. Grannie kissed Mr. Baker and the kids, then she gave Terry the cape. "I have to show Mom," said Terry, delighted. She ran from the room, trailing the cape on the floor behind her.

"I'm finished," said Collette, bringing the peeled sweet potatoes over to the counter. "Can I go change now?"

"Sure," said Mr. Baker. "Thanks for helping."

On her way upstairs, Collette passed the dining room. Sliding wooden doors usually sealed it from the rest of the house.

Mr. Baker, who was a teacher at Wild Falls College, did his reading, and graded his papers in there.

Today the doors had been pushed back. "Oh, wow!" Collette murmured as she looked inside. Mr. Baker's school papers were neatly stacked to the side. A lace tablecloth covered the table.

Mrs. Baker was setting the table. She'd piled her blonde hair on top of her head in a pretty, loose bun. She wore a navy blue dress with a lace collar.

Kenny sat at the end of the table by Mrs. Baker. He was neatly dressed in a sweater and pants. His dark wavy hair had been combed to the side.

Collette stepped into the room and picked up a white plate with gold trim. "Where did these come from?"

"They belonged to Dad's great-grandmother," said Mrs. Baker. "Grannie just gave them to us last week."

Collette picked up one of the glasses. It

was so delicate she was afraid it might break in her hand. Grandma Dupré had also had beautiful dishes and glasses.

Mrs. Baker looked at the table and seemed very pleased. "It's nice to have things handed down," she said. "I often wish I had something from my family." Mrs. Baker had been an orphan, herself. Unlike Collette, Mrs. Baker didn't even know who her parents were.

That made Collette think of something. "What happened to my grandma's things?" she asked.

"Gee, sweetheart. I don't know," Mrs. Baker admitted. "Maybe we can get Grannie to find out from her friend in New Orleans."

"Okay," said Collette, putting down the glass. "This all looks so beautiful."

"It just looks blurry to me," said Kenny sadly. Suddenly he pounded the table. "I want to see it all clearly!" he shouted angrily.

Mrs. Baker put her arm around him and stroked his hair. "I know you do, sweetie," she said softly.

Collette didn't know what to say. She wished she could help Kenny. But she couldn't. "I'd better get dressed," she said quietly, leaving the dining room.

Upstairs, the kids were getting ready. "Come on!" called Olivia, rushing out the door.

Terry climbed down from her top bunk. "I'm starved," she cried, running out of the room.

Collette quickly dressed in her new red-and-yellow-plaid jumper and new red tights.

As she sat putting them on, she caught sight of herself in the mirror. Something looked wrong. Then she remembered. "Bows, not braids, on holidays." That's what Grandma Dupré always said as she tied Collette's hair into a pretty ribbon. Quickly, Collette undid her braid. Her lovely thick hair waved down to her elbows.

She dug deeply in her bottom drawer, under her pajamas. There she found a bright yellow bow wound around a hair clip. She'd brought it with her from New Orleans.

The bright yellow bow reminded her of the spiky yellow flowers on the dining room table. *Perfect,* she thought, as she clipped up her hair on one side.

She hurried downstairs and saw that everyone was gathering around the dining room table. The turkey and all the other food sat on a narrow side table. The kids were already lined up, helping themselves to the different dishes. When they were all back at their places, Mr. Baker said grace. "Before we eat, let's all go around the table and tell one thing we're thankful for," he said.

Howie groaned. "Do we have to?"

"Yes," said Mr. Baker. "You start."

Howie thought a moment. "I'm thankful that they moved *Ninja: Master of Kung Fu* back to eight o'clock so that it's not past my bedtime anymore."

"Me, too," said Kevin.

"I'm thankful that I passed algebra," said Chris.

"I'm thankful that I live here now," said Patty.

"I thank heavens that Patty isn't as geeky as I thought she was at first," said Hilary. "Since I *have* to share a room with someone, I guess I could have done worse."

"Thanks loads, Hilary," said Patty.

"You're welcome," replied Hilary with a warm smile.

"I'm thankful for the United States Space Program," said Olivia.

"I'm happy I'm in kindergarten," said Jack.

"I'm glad nobody calls me by my real name, Desdemona," Dixie said. "Dixie is better. But I really wish my name was Jessica. Jessica or Cinderella."

"I'm thankful for the new ice skates I got for my birthday," said Terry.

"I'm happy that the Wild Falls junior high football team finally won a game," said Mark. "This is the first game we won in three years."

"I give thanks for all of you," Mrs. Baker said.

"Me, too," agreed Mr. Baker.

"I'm glad we have this good-smelling turkey," said Collette with a smile.

Then came Kenny's turn. At first he paused. Then he spoke. "I'm thankful that I'm not in some school for the blind."

There was an uncomfortable silence. Grannie broke it. "Here's what I'm thankful about," she said. "I'm thankful that I went to China in September, because that's where I met Dr. Chan. He's a lovely man *and* an eye surgeon. I wrote him about Kenny and yesterday I received a reply. He'll be in New York next week and he's willing to examine Kenny to see if the operation is necessary."

Grannie looked at Mr. Baker. "What do you say, Tom? It's time to do something. Dr. Chan is a world-famous surgeon. And he wrote that he'll do the operation for a fraction of his usual fee."

"Okay, then. I guess we're going to see Dr. Chan," said Mr. Baker.

"Thanks," Mrs. Baker said to Grannie.

"You're welcome," said Grannie. "Now let's eat!"

6

The Trip to New York

OLIVIA THREW open the front door and blew an imaginary horn. "Da-ta-da!" She smiled and held out her arm toward the door. "Behold, the star of our Christmas play. The world-famous Collette!"

"Stop it, Olivia," Collette said, embarrassed and pleased at once.

"The star?" asked Mrs. Baker, who had come to the hallway.

"Yep, she's playing Scrooge," said Olivia.

The other kids began to tromp in the

door. It was bitter and windy out. Their faces were red with cold. "Ms. Sherman was only letting boys try out for the Scrooge part," said Patty, unwrapping her scarf. "But Collette said it wasn't fair. So she tried out and got the part."

"Good for you," said Mrs. Baker proudly.

"Thanks," said Collette.

"I don't see why you would want to play an ugly, mean old man," Hilary commented as she blew on her cold, red fingers, trying to warm them.

"He happens to be the star of the whole show," said Olivia.

"Yeah, Hilary," Howie added. "You should talk. You're a boy."

"Don't remind me," Hilary sighed. "Once Collette gave Ms. Sherman the idea that girls could play boy parts, she went wild. I can't believe Alice Birmingham got the part of Scrooge's girlfriend and made *me* Tiny Tim! I'm going to die of embarrassment."

"I'm Scrooge's housekeeper," said Olivia. "I already know my line. 'Goodnight, Mr. Scrooge. And a Merry Christmas to ye.' "

After hanging up their coats the kids came into the living room. Kenny sat on the couch, his leg up on the coffee table. "How are you feeling?" Chris asked.

"Better," said Kenny. This morning he'd stayed home from school, saying he didn't feel well.

"You should have come to school," said Collette. "I bet you could have gotten the Tiny Tim part."

"I wish you had!" cried Hilary. "I don't think you were even sick. You just didn't want to try out."

"I'm too big to play Tiny Tim," said Kenny.

"No you're not," Collette insisted. "Al Hermann is Bob Cratchit, Tiny Tim's father." Al was the tallest kid in the class. "I'm taller than you are, too."

"Who cares? I have more important

things to think about," Kenny snapped. He turned his face toward the back of the couch and sulked. Collette couldn't remember Kenny ever being so grouchy. He was very unhappy, and nothing seemed to help.

"Oh, man!" cried Collette. "I'd better hurry up. Kenny, when are we leaving?" Today was the day the Bakers were taking Kenny to New York to see Dr. Chan. Mr. and Mrs. Baker said one kid could come along. They'd drawn names from a hat to see who it would be. Collette's name had been picked.

"As soon as Dad gets home from school," Kenny mumbled.

Collette charged up the stairs. Quickly she packed a few things in her flowered overnight bag. They were taking a train because Mr. Baker said it would be too hard to park a van in the city.

Collette ran down the stairs to the hallway.

"I see you're ready," said Grannie Baker as she came in the front door.

"I'm so excited. Have you ever been to New York City before?" Collette asked.

"I was born there," Grannie replied. "It's a grand city."

Finally, Mr. Baker rushed in the door. "Let's go," he said. "We want to catch the six o'clock express."

"We're all set," said Mrs. Baker, coming in from the kitchen. "I packed our suitcase, but maybe I should stay here. I can't leave Chris with all these kids."

"*MO*-ther!" moaned Chris from the stairs. "Stop worrying. I can handle it."

"Okay, but I've left a list of phone numbers on the refrigerator door," said Mrs. Baker. "Promise to call if anything at all should — "

Mr. Baker was helping Kenny get his coat on. "Ann, we have to leave," he said.

"All right, I'm coming," she answered.

Finally, Mr. and Mrs. Baker, Grannie,

Kenny, and Collette got into the van and drove to the train station. Mr. Baker dropped them at the station, then went off to park the van in a lot.

A shrill whistle announced the approaching train. "Where is Dad?" asked Kenny nervously.

Huffing and puffing, Mr. Baker ran toward them. "Come on, we'll buy tickets on the train," he said. "On my back, son," he said, squatting in front of Kenny. "You won't make it up those stairs to the train platform."

"I feel like a baby," Kenny grumbled, wrapping his free arm around his father's neck. When Kenny was on, they all hurried up the stairs to the train.

Soon they were traveling down the railroad line. Collette gazed out the window. The train ran alongside the wide Hudson River. A full moon shed its silvery light on the water. It seemed so magical to Collette.

Kenny sat beside her. He craned his

neck to look out the window. "What can you see?" Collette asked him.

"Just darkness," he replied. "There's something bright, too. I guess that's the moon, right?"

"Right," Collette answered. "Don't worry. You'll see again soon."

"I'm scared," Kenny whispered.

Collette held his hand and squeezed. "Grannie says this guy is the best."

"I hope so," sighed Kenny.

By the time the train pulled into the station in New York City, Kenny was asleep. "We're here," Collette said, shoving him lightly.

Mr. Baker helped Kenny off the train. Grand Central Station was busy with people scurrying in all directions. Collette had never seen so many different kinds of people. "Why are they all rushing around?" she asked Grannie.

"Everyone in New York rushes," Grannie answered. "That's how it is in all big cities."

Out on the street, a light snow was falling. Collette blinked at the bright lights. She strained her neck trying to see to the very tops of the tall buildings. And the sounds! Horns honked. Music played from stores. People shouted.

Mr. Baker stood by the curb, waving his hand. A cab stopped, and the family piled in. "The West Side Arms, on Broadway and Fifty-fourth," Mr. Baker told the cab driver.

The driver dropped them off in front of a plain brick building with an awning. The snow whipped around them as they entered.

The lobby was small but elegant. A blue velvet couch sat behind a dark wood coffee table. Colorful flowers stood in tall vases.

"Baker, two rooms," Mr. Baker said to the man behind the desk.

"Very good, sir," said the man. "Sign here."

A bellhop came and took their suitcases. They followed him to their rooms on the fifteenth floor. Collette pulled back the heavy tan curtains. Below, the people hurried about like small ants. The cars inched along the crowded street. *New York City is certainly different from Wild Falls,* thought Collette.

Kenny snapped on the TV and lay on the bed. Collette could tell that he was listening and not watching since he stared at the ceiling.

"Tomorrow is the big day, son," said Mr. Baker. "How do you feel?"

"Horrible," said Kenny. "Can we go home?"

7

Dr. Chan

THE BAKERS didn't go home. Mr. Baker said that they had already come too far. "It's okay to be scared," he told Kenny.

Kenny didn't say anything at first. "But what if it doesn't work?" he asked after a while.

"Dr. Chan is one of the best in the world," Grannie assured him. "He'll know what to do."

"That's why we're here," added Mrs. Baker.

In the morning they got up early. "It's

still snowing," said Collette, looking out the hotel window. She couldn't get used to being up so high. She thought it was thrilling and wonderful.

The entire trip seemed wonderful to her. She loved eating breakfast in the diner. Two Indian men, their heads wrapped in white turbans, sat in the booth behind them.

At the counter was a man whose skin was even darker than her own dark skin. His black hair fell in long braids down his back.

"Why don't we have so many different kinds of people in Wild Falls?" she asked as the family ate their breakfast. "In Wild Falls we're the most different family in town. Here, nobody even notices us."

"Big cities attract people from all over the world," said Grannie. "Lots of folks come here to study and to work."

"Let's move to the city," Collette suggested.

"It's not easy to have so many kids in the city," said Mrs. Baker. "You couldn't have a yard of your own and you'd be much more crowded in an apartment."

"I don't want to live here," said Kenny. "It's too noisy. There are too many people."

"Well, I'm moving here when I grow up," said Collette.

Grannie patted her hand. "Maybe you will," she said.

They took a cab to a group of shiny, modern buildings that took up more than one block. Grannie led them to the right building and the elevator.

They rang a doorbell and the door was answered by a Chinese woman in a white nurse's uniform. She led them into an empty waiting room and, in a few moments, a short, plump man with white hair and glasses came out of his office. It was Dr. Chan. "Amelia," he said, greeting Grannie by her first name. "What a great pleasure it is to see you again."

Grannie introduced her family and

soon Dr. Chan took Kenny into his office for an examination. The nurse went in with them. The Bakers waited outside for over an hour.

Finally, Dr. Chan invited them into the office. Collette sat down on a couch next to Kenny while the adults sat in chairs around the desk. Dr. Chan said some medical things about blocked blood vessels and blood leakage. Collette couldn't really understand it all. It seemed that if Kenny's eyes hadn't improved by now, they weren't going to. Not without an operation.

"It is not an especially difficult operation, but it *is* a very delicate area," said Dr. Chan. "If you wish, I will gladly do the surgery."

"That would make me feel much better," said Mr. Baker.

"Will it hurt?" Kenny asked suddenly.

"There is always some discomfort," Dr. Chan said honestly. "But we will give you something to make you sleep during the operation. There will be no great pain."

"Is the operation sure to work?" asked Mrs. Baker.

"No operation is one-hundred percent sure," Dr. Chan replied. "But this one has a high success rate. I can perform the surgery two weeks from today."

The Bakers said they would be there. Mr. Baker helped Kenny as they walked to the elevator. "You're in the hands of an expert. Pretty soon you'll have your sight back again," Mr. Baker said.

"Good. I'm sick of all this blurriness," said Kenny hopefully.

Both Kenny and Grannie slept on the train ride back. Collette dozed with her head leaning against the window. But she wasn't really asleep and she could hear what her parents were saying.

"This trip cost more than I expected," said Mr. Baker. "We don't have the money for another one."

"We have the Christmas money," said Mrs. Baker. "Would that do it?"

"Sure, but that means no Christmas presents. I hate to do that to the kids."

"The kids will understand. I'll manage to get a little something for Dixie and Jack," said Mrs. Baker. "We have no other choice."

No presents! Collette's jaw dropped. This was terrible! Collette had been counting on getting a bike for Christmas. Her bike was too small. The seat had been raised as far as it would go, and by spring she might even be taller.

Her birthday wasn't until August. That meant that the whole spring and summer would pass without her having a bike of her own.

She wanted to jump up and tell her parents it was no fair.

But how could she do that? It would be so selfish.

Little snores came from Kenny as he napped beside her. She loved all her brothers and sisters, even Hilary. (Though she didn't always *like* Hilary.) But, after

Olivia, she felt closest to Kenny. He was nice and funny. And he always stuck up for his brothers and sisters in school.

Now it was their turn to stick up for him.

Collette looked out the window. Although it was still light, she could see the faint trace of the moon in the sky. It wasn't as fat or full as it had been on Friday night. But it was definitely there in the darkening, purplish-blue sky.

Close to the moon, a star twinkled faintly. *A star!* Collette sat up straighter. How could she have forgotten the magic wishing star? That was how she would get her bike.

Every year, on the twentieth of December, Collette wished on the star nearest the moon. Grandma Dupré had told her it was a magic Christmas wishing star. Only Grandma Dupré ever got to know what she had wished for.

Every year Collette's wish had come true.

This had been going on ever since she

could remember. Even before her parents died, Grandma Dupré spent Christmasses with them. She would call up on the twentieth without fail and ask what Collette had wished for. "Now don't tell another person," Grandma would say. "Only you, I, and the star must know."

Collette wondered if the wishing star would work now that Grandma Dupré was gone. Yes, she decided, it would.

She leaned back against the seat and thought. Maybe she should wish for presents for everyone. But she wasn't so sure that would work. "Tell the wishing star the one thing that you want most," Grandma Dupré had said. "The wishing star can't handle a zillion little wishes. Only one big wish."

Last year she'd wanted an electronic game system. She knew it was too expensive to get any other way. On Christmas morning, there it was. By the end of the day, Grandma Dupré shook her head and said she'd have to have a talk with the wishing star next year. The electronic boops and beeps were driving her crazy.

Collette decided she would share her bike with whomever wanted it. She didn't like the idea, but that would be the only way she could feel right about having a bike when no one else had gotten a present. It was better to have a bike they could share than nothing at all.

"Next stop, Wild Falls," announced the conductor.

Kenny's eyes fluttered open. "Are we home yet?"

"Almost," replied Collette as the train chugged into the station. Suddenly Collette remembered something. "I'm supposed to have three pages of lines memorized by Monday," she told Kenny. "Oh, man! I'll have to spend all day tomorrow studying lines."

"That's what you get for being the star of the play," Kenny teased.

8

Collette's Plan

COLLETTE WRIGGLED her nose. Ms. Sherman had decided that Scrooge should have a bushy white mustache. "We have to make you look like a mean old man," she'd said.

"Yes, yes, perfect," said Ms. Sherman, pressing the mustache down flat on Collette's lips. Collette stood on the stage with the other students who would be in the play. The teachers were getting costumes ready.

Patty, Olivia, Terry, and Howie were nearby, being fitted for costumes. Collette looked over at Hilary and smiled to herself. Hilary was dressed in short pants, knee socks, and a vest. Ms. Allen, the second-grade teacher, was tucking Hilary's long hair into a big cap.

It wasn't the costume that made Collette smile. It was the look on Hilary's face. Hilary was totally disgusted with her outfit.

Down below the stage, Mr. Popol was playing the piano. The chorus of second- and third-graders was practicing holiday songs. Right now they were singing "Jingle Bells."

Suddenly, Mr. Popol stopped playing. "Someone is way, way off-key," he said. He asked a few different kids to stand and sing alone. They sounded all right to Collette.

Then he asked Kenny to sing.

"Dashing through the sno-o-o-o-o," Kenny croaked.

Collette cringed. Hilary caught her eye. She mouthed the words, "I told you."

"Listen, Kenny," said Mr. Popol. He played and sang. Mr. Popol had a beautiful, warm rich voice. "Try it like that."

"Dashing through the sn-o-o-o-o," Kenny sang, just as badly as he had before. Collette felt terrible for him. She knew he was embarrassed.

"*Snow*, Kenny," said Mr. Popol. "Don't drag it out. Sing it quickly. Try again."

"Dash-i-i-ing thr-o-o-o the snow," Kenny tried it again.

"Hmmmmmm," mused Mr. Popol. "Sing softly for now. We'll work on it together later."

That was when Collette came up with her idea. She would have to talk to Hilary, though. Like it or not, she'd need Hilary's help.

Collette found her chance later that night. "I have to talk to you about something important," she said, coming into the room Patty and Hilary shared.

Patty and Hilary were lying on their beds. Patty was studying her lines for the play. Hilary was reading a fashion magazine.

"Well, what is it?" asked Hilary.

"Do you really not want to be in the play?" Collette asked her. "Really and truly?"

"If I could be Scrooge's girlfriend, I'd want to be in the play," said Hilary. "But there is no way I am going to appear on stage dressed like a boy. A boy with a crutch! I am just not going to be in it. That's all there is to it."

"Did you tell Ms. Sherman?" Patty asked.

Hilary smiled wickedly. "I have a better plan. I'm not going to learn my lines. Then Ms. Sherman will get so upset she'll give the part to someone else."

"Oh, man, you have nerve," said Collette. "Aren't you worried about getting into trouble?"

Hillary's smile faded. "A little," she admitted. "But I am *not* going to be seen dressed as a boy."

Collette climbed onto Hilary's bed. "I know a way that you can get out of the play and not get into trouble, either."

"Yeah?" asked Hilary, her eyes lighting eagerly.

"We can get Kenny to help you with your lines. That way he'll learn them. Then, on the night of the play, you pretend to be sick. Kenny will be the only one who knows the lines and he can go on for you."

"What good will that do Kenny?" asked Patty.

"For one thing, he won't have to sing," Collette explained. "And it will cheer him up. Everyone said he was good in the play last year."

"He was pretty funny," Hilary agreed.

"He's been so sad lately," said Collette. "Singing in the chorus is only going to make him feel worse. But being onstage, with everyone clapping, might make him happy."

"But what if he goes bumping into everything?" asked Hilary doubtfully.

"He'll have had his operation by then," Collette reminded her. "Besides, Tiny Tim is supposed to have crutches."

"What if the operation doesn't work?" said Hilary.

"It's going to work," Collette snapped.

"Okay, okay. Cool out," said Hilary. "I'll give it a try. I'll do anything as long as I don't have to be Tiny Tim."

"Great. Let's go find Kenny," said Collette. Hilary grabbed her script from the dresser and followed Collette out of the room.

They found Kenny in his bedroom. He shared the room with Howie and Kevin, but they were downstairs watching *Ninja Master*. "Hey, Kenny, we need your help," said Collette, knocking on the open door. "Hilary is having trouble with her lines.

The way she says them is all wrong. Could you help us?"

Kenny shut off the tape he'd been listening to. "Why do you need me to help?"

"Oh, come on, Kenny. You're good at this stuff," said Hilary. "You didn't forget a single line when you were Father Christmas. The principal herself said you'd be a fine actor someday. Remember?"

"Yeah, she did say that," Kenny recalled proudly.

"So, will you help us?" Collette pressed.

Kenny shrugged. "I don't have anything else to do."

Hilary began reading her lines. Collette read all the other parts. When they were done, they asked Kenny what he thought. "You're not awful," he said. "You're horrible."

"You don't have to be insulting," huffed Hilary. "Just tell me how to do them better."

"For one thing, you say your lines like you hate Scrooge. Everybody else hates

him, but you're supposed to like the guy,"
Kenny began.

"What kind of an idiot likes Scrooge?"
Hilary argued.

"I don't know!" cried Kenny. "I didn't
write the play. But Tiny Tim is this dumb
little kid. He likes everybody. He doesn't
know any better, I guess."

"I don't know how to do that," Hilary
sulked.

"Like this," said Kenny. "What's your
first line?"

"Let's invite Mr. Scrooge to Christmas
dinner," Hilary said, rolling her eyes.

"See? You said that as if it was a stupid
idea and you knew it," Kenny told her.
"It's supposed to be more like, 'Hey, I have
a really great idea! Let's invite Mr. Scrooge
to dinner.' "

"That's not the line," Hilary corrected
primly.

"I know, but that's the *feeling* of the
line," said Kenny. "Tell me the next line."

Hilary read it. Kenny told her how it

should be said. He went over every single line with her. At times, Collette had to force herself not to laugh. Hilary would purposely make mistakes just so Kenny would go over a line again and again. Hilary really knew how to drive a person crazy — but she was making sure Kenny learned the part.

"Do you think we could do this again tomorrow night?" Hilary asked when they were done.

"If you want to," Kenny agreed. "I should find someone to teach *me* to sing."

"Don't worry," said Collette. "You'll be fine."

Collette was very happy with the way her plan was turning out. She was sure it was going to work.

9

The Wishing Night

"SO LONG!"

"Good luck!"

"We love you!"

The Bakers stood on the train platform under a dark snowy sky. All but Dixie and Jack — who were home with Grannie — had come to say good-bye. They waved and shouted to Kenny and Mr. Baker as they boarded the train. Kenny was going to the city for his operation.

The train pulled out and the family headed back to the van. "I sure hope this works," said Olivia, pulling up her hood against the wind.

"It had better," said Hilary. "Especially since we gave up Christmas because of it."

"You didn't give up Christmas, Hilary," said Chris. "You gave up presents."

"What's the difference?" asked Howie as he wiped snow from his glasses.

"Christmas is about loving each other," Chris said. "You give presents to show your love. But if you don't have presents, you can show your love in other ways."

"We could make stuff for each other," Terry suggested.

"Pul-lease," moaned Hilary. "You mean geeky stuff like pot holders and knitted headbands?"

"I like knitted headbands," said Patty.

"You would," mumbled Hilary.

"We could give things we already have," Mark suggested, looking at Howie slyly. "Like, if someone wants a ball or something you have, you could give it to him."

"Forget it!" yelped Howie. "You are not

getting my autographed baseball. No way."

"Nice Christmas spirit, Howie," Mark grumbled. "Real nice."

Howie grinned. "Just call me Mr. Grinch. But you are not getting that ball."

"I don't like that idea, either," Hilary sided with Howie.

"Of course you don't," said Olivia. "You've already borrowed everything you want and stuck it in your drawer. That reminds me. I haven't seen my bunny slippers lately."

Collette listened to her brothers and sisters and she worried about her bike. Up in the sky, white snow clouds covered the moon. Today was the twentieth of December. It was time to make her wish. Could she still wish on a star, even if she couldn't see it?

She decided to wait. Maybe it would come out later.

The kids were unusually quiet as Mrs. Baker drove them back to the house. It was as though all of them were wrapped in their own private thoughts.

That evening, Collette kept looking out the window. Clouds still covered the sky.

When she finally went to bed, she couldn't sleep. She shared a room with Terry and Olivia. She slept on the bottom bunk, Terry slept on the top. Olivia had a single bed across the room.

"Olivia?" Collette whispered in the dark.

There was no answer. Olivia was already asleep.

"Terry?" She was asleep, too.

Collette got up and checked the window. Still cloudy.

She pulled a chair up to the window. With her head resting on her arms, she stared out. *A pink bike with a banana seat and tassles,* she decided. Then she changed her mind. *No, a blue racer. An English racer.*

Collette didn't mean to, but she fell asleep there at the window.

She dreamed of Kenny. He was laughing and doing somersaults in the air. One time he landed and he was dressed as Father Christmas. The second time he landed, he was dressed as Tiny Tim. His eyes sparkled with mischief the way they used to. He threw away his Tiny Tim crutch and danced a happy jig.

Collette awakened with a start. Rubbing her eyes, she looked up at the sky. The clouds had all been swept away. Stars twinkled against the blue-black sky. A thin crescent moon sat high above her. At its bottom tip a star sparkled. There it was — the magic wishing star.

"Wishing star," Collette whispered, closing her eyes. "Please give me the thing I want most. Make Kenny all better. Make his operation work."

10

Disappointments

ON THE MONDAY after his operation, Kenny came home. Dr. Chan had taken the bandages off his eyes that morning.

His vision was still blurry.

"Give it time," Dr. Chan told Mr. Baker. "His sight should improve in the next two days. If it does not, this might be more serious than I thought. Unfortunately, I return to China tonight. My associate, Dr. Lee, will be available, should any problems arise."

"Some Christmas Eve this is," Hilary

mumbled. "No presents and Kenny still can't see."

"Shhhhhhh," hissed Collette. "He'll hear you. He feels bad enough already."

They were in the living room putting tinsel on the tall tree. Mr. Baker had cut the tree himself, and it almost reached the ceiling. On top sat a beautiful shimmering star.

Collette looked up at the star and wondered what had gone wrong. Why hadn't the magic wishing star granted her wish?

You're such a baby, she told herself. *There's no such thing as a wishing star! Grandma Dupré made it up.* Of course! Why hadn't she realized it before? She always told Grandma what she'd wished. It was Grandma who had gotten her all those things.

How could you be so dumb? she scolded herself. *What a jerk!*

"Come on! Everybody who is in the play has to be at school by six," Mrs. Baker called.

"I don't feel good," Hilary said to Collette.

"Forget it," said Collette. "Kenny can't go on for you now. He can't see well enough. The plan is off."

"I'm not kidding," said Hilary. "My stomach really hurts."

"Get off it, okay?" snapped Collette. She was in no mood for Hilary's nonsense. "You have to go on. Everyone is counting on you."

Collette went to join her brothers and sisters as they put on their jackets in the hallway. Mr. Baker was already warming up the van. Chris helped Kenny button his jacket around his cast. His collarbone and rib had healed, but his arm and leg were still bandaged. "You guys will all be great tonight," Chris said.

"I won't," said Kenny glumly. "I'm not even going to open my mouth."

"Ah, come on," said Patty. "Just sing. It'll come out okay."

"I feel sick," said Hilary.

"You make me feel sick, too," laughed Howie.

"It's just butterflies in your stomach," Olivia told her.

"Eewwww! Hilary has butterflies in her tummy!" cried Dixie, horrified at the idea.

"Olivia means Hilary is nervous," Patty explained.

"I'm not nervous — I feel sick," insisted Hilary.

"You'll be fine," said Chris. "You'd better hurry."

The kids got in the van and Mr. Baker dropped them off at school. They all changed into their costumes. Ms. Sherman stuck Collette's braid into the back of her shirt; then she stuck a white wig over the rest of Collette's hair. Collette needed her real hair to be dark, so that she could play the young Scrooge in act two.

"Wow! You look great," Olivia told Collette. Olivia's dark curls peeked out from a soft, cloth bonnet. She wore a long skirt and a blouse with puffed sleeves.

"So do you," answered Collette.

"Where's Hilary?" Olivia asked.

Collette looked around, but didn't see her. "Uh-oh, this gives me a bad feeling," she said.

"Me, too," Olivia agreed. "She said she wouldn't be in this play no matter what."

"Maybe she's in the bathroom," Patty suggested hopefully.

The girls went down the hall to check. "Hilary?" Terry called, poking her head in the door.

All they heard was an awful, retching sound coming from one of the booths. They rushed to the booth. "Oh, no!" cried Olivia.

There, hanging over the toilet bowl, was Hilary. And she was throwing up.

Olivia gathered back Hilary's long hair and waited for her to stop throwing up. "I told you I was sick," muttered Hilary when she was done.

"How do you feel now?" asked Collette, handing her a piece of toilet tissue.

"A little better, but — " Hilary suddenly became very white. Then she was sick all over again.

"She can't go on," Olivia said. "We have to tell Ms. Sherman."

Olivia waited with Hilary while Collette ran and found Ms. Sherman. "Oh, dear, dear, dear," mumbled Ms. Sherman, hurrying toward the bathroom. "Now what are we going to do?"

"Our brother Kenny knows the part," Collette blurted out. "He even has his own crutch."

Ms. Sherman stopped. "But isn't he having trouble seeing?"

"Yes, but I'll be on the stage with him some of the time," said Collette. "And Al can help him. Bob Cratchit is always lugging Tiny Tim around, anyway."

"Would Kenny do it?" asked Ms. Sherman.

"I don't know," Collette answered honestly.

Ms. Sherman helped Hilary out of the

bathroom. Then she called Patty. "Wait backstage with Hilary until your parents arrive," Ms. Sherman told her.

"You must be so disappointed," Ms. Sherman said to Hilary.

"It's really all right," said Hilary, holding her hand over her mouth and looking very green.

Ms. Sherman asked Mr. Popol's permission to take Kenny out of the chorus. "Fine with me," said Mr. Popol, sounding relieved.

Ms. Sherman asked Kenny to play the part of Tiny Tim.

"I'm not sure I know the lines," he said.

"Sure you do. You say them great," Collette pointed out. "You *have* to do it. The whole class needs you."

"I'll try," said Kenny, leaning on his crutch.

"All right, Kenny!" cried Collette happily.

Soon it was time for the play. Collette had been too busy to be nervous. But now, as the lights dimmed, her stomach flip-flopped. She breathed deeply. *You'll be fine,* she said to herself. Last night Olivia had gone over the lines with her. She knew them all perfectly.

The curtain came up, and Collette stepped onto the stage. "There she is!" cried a voice from the audience. It was Dixie. Collette tried not to pay attention. She said her lines and things went very well.

The second act was at the home of Bob Cratchit. Kenny stood in the wings. Collette saw that his hands were shaking. "Don't worry — you'll be great," she told him.

Al Hermann came up alongside them. "Just kind of lean on me," he told Kenny.

"Good luck," whispered Collette as Kenny hopped along beside Al.

Suddenly, *crash! Smash!* Kenny's crutch knocked over a chair and sent it tumbling to the ground.

11

Wishes Come True

"OH, TINY TIM," said Ellie Pringle, who was playing Mrs. Cratchit. "You are always knocking things over."

"Leave our son alone," said Al, helping Kenny to another chair. "It's bad enough he can't walk. Now he's broken his arm, too. Give the kid a break."

"I've had too many breaks already," joked Kenny. "I have a broken arm and a broken leg. But seriously, I'm all excited about Christmas."

By now, the audience was laughing happily. The rest of the play went perfectly. Well, almost. Alice Birmingham got her dress caught on a nail in the stage and ripped it. And the ghost of Christmas Future tripped over his long, black robe. But the audience didn't seem to mind.

And Kenny was fantastic. He seemed more and more confident as he moved around the stage. Finally, he had to speak the last line of the play. "God bless us, every one!" He shouted it loudly and cheerfully.

The audience clapped wildly. Some of them stood up. The students held hands and took their bows. Ms. Sherman came onstage and handed Collette a small bouquet of white roses. She had Collette take a special, extra bow.

Then the chorus came onstage and began singing Christmas carols. Mr. Popol asked the audience to sing along. The kids who'd been in the play all sat in the front rows, where the chorus had sat during the play.

Collette couldn't remember the last time she'd felt this happy. Everyone smiled at her. She knew she'd done well.

Kenny sat in front of her. "You were great," she whispered to him.

He turned in his chair and his face was lit with a smile. "Collette," he whispered. "You're not blurry. Not at all."

"What!" cried Collette.

"In the middle of the play, I noticed things were getting better. I can see you fine!"

Collette forgot where she was, or what was happening around her. She jumped to her feet in the middle of "Frosty the Snowman."

"Mom! Dad!" she cried, looking around the audience for her parents.

Mr. Popol stopped playing. Mr. and Mrs. Baker rushed up the aisle. "What's the matter?" asked Mrs. Baker frantically.

"Nothing's the matter!" cried Collette. "Kenny can see."

"It worked!" yelled Mr. Baker. "The operation worked!"

The entire audience clapped. Mr. Popol began to play once again. But he switched songs. He played "Joy to the World." The chorus and audience joined in.

Collette thought her heart would explode with joy.

Later, out in the parking lot, the family was giddy with happiness. Mr. Baker carried Kenny on his shoulders. They sang Christmas carols all the way home.

When they pulled up to the house, it looked warm and inviting. An electric candle lit the window of each room.

The family was greeted by the smells of a fire in the fireplace and hot cider warming in the kitchen.

They told Grannie about Kenny. She hugged him tight. "That's my boy," she said. "That's my brave boy."

"How's Hilary?" asked Mrs. Baker. Mr. Baker had brought her home before returning to the play.

"She's sleeping, poor dear," said Grannie, wiping the tears of happiness from her eyes. "I think it's just a case of the flu. No need to worry."

The family sat near the fire and drank their hot cider. After a while, Mr. and Mrs. Baker tucked them all in.

Collette fell asleep right away, but some noise downstairs woke her. She crept to the stairway and looked down.

Her parents were laughing and helping Grannie put some gifts under the tree. There were twelve packages wrapped in beautiful paper. "Thanks, Mom," said Mr. Baker. "This will make Christmas brighter."

"No problemo," laughed Grannie. "I have this holiday spirit thing under control." Suddenly Grannie spotted Collette peering over the bannister. "Hey, is that an elf I see?" she teased.

"You should be sleeping," said Mrs. Baker kindly.

"I heard noises," said Collette.

"Come down for a few minutes," said Mrs. Baker. "I have something to show you."

Collette came down the stairs as Mrs. Baker took a big cardboard box from the hall closet and pushed it out onto the floor. "Grannie contacted her friend in New Orleans, the one who knew your grandmother," said Mrs. Baker. "This box came in the mail today."

Mrs. Baker opened the box. Inside were lace tablecloths, books, plates and glasses, a worn photo album, a flowered shawl, and a shiny black jewelry box.

"These are your grandmother's things," said Mrs. Baker, handing Collette the jewelry box. "I can put most of it in the attic for you, but I thought you might like to have this now."

As Collette lifted the lid, the box played a song. She didn't know the words, yet she remembered the tune. Grandma Dupré had often hummed it.

The box held old-fashioned but lovely pieces of jewelry. Collette picked up a gold locket and opened it. The locket held a picture of Collette as a toddler.

"It's like she sent me a Christmas present," said Collette.

"It sure is," said Mr. Baker, who had come into the hallway.

Mrs. Baker stroked Collette's hair. "Think you can sleep?" she asked. "It's getting late."

Collette nodded. "Goodnight," she said, kissing her parents. Holding her jewelry box, she padded softly back to her bedroom. What a day this had been! What a wonderful day.

Back in their bedroom, Olivia and Terry slept. Collette smiled, seeing that Olivia still wore her bonnet from the play. A smear of eyeliner was left on Olivia's cheek.

Collette wandered to the window. The stars twinkled merrily in the black sky.

Collette found the star closest to the moon.

A thought came to her, and somehow she was sure it was true.

She knew that Grandma Dupré had always made her Christmas wishes come true. And this year — somehow — she had done it again.

Collette set the box on the floor and put her hand to the cold window. She tried to touch the star. "Merry Christmas, Grandma," she whispered.

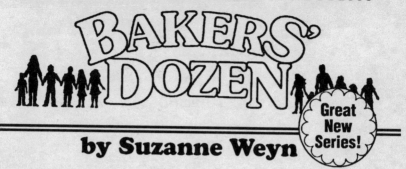